The
Tapping Tale

The Tapping Tale

Judy Giglio
Illustrated by Joe Cepeda

Green Light Readers
Harcourt, Inc.
Orlando   Austin   New York   San Diego   London

Pat ran to see Ronda.

At last, Ronda was spending the night!

"Mom, Ronda is here."

Pat and Ronda played all day.

At last, it was time to sleep.

It was dark in Pat's room.

"What's that tapping?" asked Ronda.

TAP!

TAP!

TAP!

TAP!

TAP!

TAP!

TAP!

TAP!

TAP!

TAP!

"I can look in the hall," said Pat.

"Look!" said Ronda.
"This is what's tapping."

"I think it's a tail!" said Ronda.

"Oh, that's Rip!" said Pat.
"Rip, hop up here."

"Rip is happy to see you," said Pat.

"Oh, Rip," said Ronda. "This is better.
You can sleep up here!"

Guess My Pet!

**You have met Pat's pet dog, Rip.
Write a riddle about a pet you know.**

WHAT YOU'LL NEED

paper   **pen or pencil**

1. Think of a pet.

2. Write three clues about the pet.

3. Trade clues with a friend.

It is green.

It eats bugs.

It is smaller than a book.

4. Read the clues.

5. Try to guess the animal!

Meet the Illustrator

Joe Cepeda reads a story many times before he works on the pictures for it. He doesn't start drawing until he knows the story well. First he draws the place where the story happens. He draws the people last. He likes to make the characters look like people he really knows!

Requests for permission to make copies of any part of the work should be submitted
online at www.harcourt.com/contact or mailed to the following address:
Permissions Department, Houghton Mifflin Harcourt Publishing Company,
6277 Sea Harbor Drive, Orlando, Florida 32887-6777.

www.HarcourtBooks.com

First Green Light Readers edition 2000
Green Light Readers is a trademark of Harcourt, Inc., registered in the
United States of America and/or other jurisdictions.

The Library of Congress has cataloged an earlier edition as follows:
Giglio, Judy.
The tapping tale/Judy Giglio; illustrated by Joe Cepeda.
p.   cm.
"Green Light Readers."
Summary: On her first sleepover, a mysterious tapping sound keeps Ronda awake.
[1. Sleepovers—Fiction.   2. Dogs—Fiction.]   I. Cepeda, Joe, ill.   II. Title.
PZ7.G366Tap   2000
[E]—dc21   99-6808
ISBN 978-0-15-204812-9
ISBN 978-0-15-204852-5 (pb)

LEO   10 9 8
4500320477

Ages 4–6
Grades: K–1
Guided Reading Level: C–D
Reading Recovery Level: 5–6

Green Light Readers
For the reader who's ready to GO!

"A must-have for any family with a beginning reader."—*Boston Sunday Herald*

"You can't go wrong with adding several copies of these terrific books to your beginning-to-read collection."—*School Library Journal*

"A winner for the beginner."—*Booklist*

Five Tips to Help Your Child Become a Great Reader

1. Get involved. Reading aloud to and with your child is just as important as encouraging your child to read independently.

2. Be curious. Ask questions about what your child is reading.

3. Make reading fun. Allow your child to pick books on subjects that interest her or him.

4. Words are everywhere—not just in books. Practice reading signs, packages, and cereal boxes with your child.

5. Set a good example. Make sure your child sees YOU reading.

Why Green Light Readers Is the Best Series for Your New Reader

- Created exclusively for beginning readers by some of the biggest and brightest names in children's books

- Reinforces the reading skills your child is learning in school

- Encourages children to read—and finish—books by themselves

- Offers extra enrichment through fun, age-appropriate activities unique to each story

- Incorporates characteristics of the Reading Recovery program used by educators

- Developed with Harcourt School Publishers and credentialed educational consultants